£1-50
(23)

# ·ABERDEEN·

## COLIN BAXTER

RICHARD DREW PUBLISHING
GLASGOW

OVERLEAF
OIL PLATFORMS
OFF ABERDEEN BAY

WIDE CONTRASTS IN THE SCENERY OF SCOTLAND ALWAYS IMPRESS THE VISITOR. WHERE ELSE CAN BE FOUND IN SO SMALL AN AREA MOUNTAINS, SAVAGE SEAS, ROUGH COASTS, WOODED VALLEYS, WILD MOORLAND, TUMBLING RIVERS AND FERTILE PLAINS? CHANGING PLAY OF LIGHT BROUGHT BY THE FICKLE CLIMATE ADDS MYSTERY TO THE SCOTTISH EXPERIENCE.

NO-ONE IN RECENT YEARS HAS CAPTURED THIS EVER-CHANGING VARIETY AS SENSITIVELY AS THE PHOTOGRAPHER, COLIN BAXTER, WHO HAS IN THIS SERIES SELECTED CERTAIN AREAS AND THEMES TO CONVEY THE RICH DIVERSITY OF SCOTLAND'S CITIES AND COUNTRYSIDE.

ALTHOUGH ONE OF SCOTLAND'S OLDEST TOWNS, ABERDEEN LOOKS TO THE FUTURE, NOT THE PAST. THE SEA HAS ALWAYS BEEN IMPORTANT TO ITS ECONOMY AND IT REMAINS A BUSY FISHING PORT, BUT ABOVE ALL IT IS THE CENTRE OF THE OIL INDUSTRY AND THIS HAS BROUGHT A NEW COSMOPOLITAN LIFE TO THE CITY.

IN KING'S COLLEGE IT HAS ONE OF THE OLDEST UNIVERSITIES IN THE BRITISH ISLES AND THE LATER PART OF THE UNIVERSITY, MARISCHAL COLLEGE IS THE SECOND-LARGEST GRANITE BUILDING IN THE WORLD, SECOND ONLY TO THE ESCORIAL IN MADRID. MOST OF THE BUILDINGS THROUGHOUT THE CITY ARE BUILT OF THIS IMPOSING STONE; THE NAME GRANITE CITY IS NO MISNOMER.

FISH MARKET QUAY
AT DAWN

CHIMNEYPOTS
AND THE KIRK OF
ST. NICHOLAS

TOWN HOUSE
AT DUSK

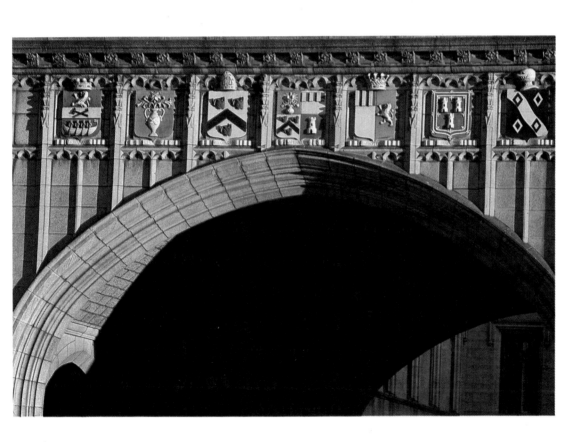

Marischal College,
University of Aberdeen

WAR MEMORIAL,
SCHOOLHILL

ABERDEEN
BEACH AND BAY

UPPER DOCK
AND FERRYHILL

TOWN HOUSE
CLOCK TOWER
FROM ROSEMOUNT
VIADUCT

TOWER ON
BUILDING OF
SALVATION ARMY
HEADQUARTERS

TOWN HOUSE, TOLBOOTH AND
MARBLE STATUE OF QUEEN VICTORIA

ABERDEEN
ART GALLERY

JAMES DUN'S HOUSE,
SCHOOLHILL

STREET LIGHT,
HIS MAJESTY'S THEATRE

SUNDIAL ON
TOWN HOUSE

Looking across
Fish Market and
Albert Basin to Torry Hill

Fish market

DOORWAY OF
TOWN HOUSE

SEAGULL AND
CHIMNEYPOTS

KING'S COLLEGE
CHAPEL,
UNIVERSITY OF
ABERDEEN,
OLD ABERDEEN

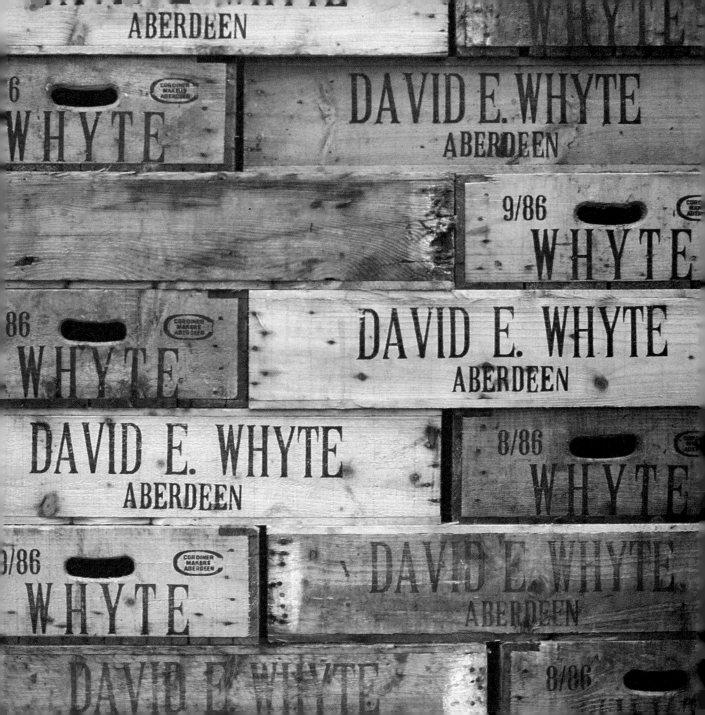

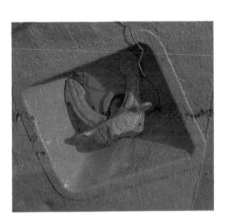

Provost Ross's House,
Aberdeen Maritime
Museum, Shiprow

CHAPEL AND CROWN TOWER,
KING'S COLLEGE,
UNIVERSITY OF ABERDEEN

TURRET,
HIGH STREET,
OLD ABERDEEN

His Majesty's Theatre

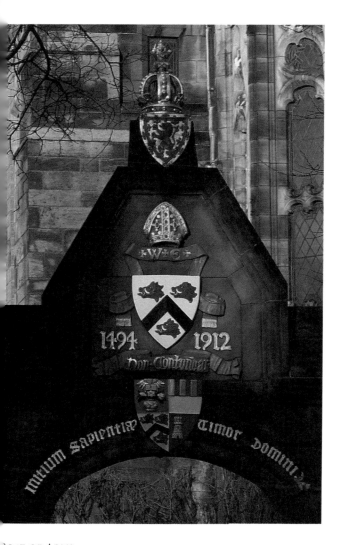

Coat of Arms,
King's College,
University of Aberdeen,
Old Aberdeen

His Majesty's Theatre
and high rise

MARISCHAL COLLEGE,
UNIVERSITY OF
ABERDEEN, AT DUSK

First Published 1987 by
RICHARD DREW PUBLISHING
6 CLAIRMONT GARDENS, GLASGOW G3 7LW, SCOTLAND

Printed and bound in Great Britain by
Blantyre Printing and Binding Co. Ltd.

British Library Cataloguing in Publication Data

"Aberdeen. – (Experience Scotland).
1. Aberdeen (Grampian) – Description –
Guide-books
I. Title      II. Series
914. 12'3504 DA890.A2

ISBN 0-86267-188-4